Small Towns, Dark Places

Tansy Undercrypt

Small Towns, Dark Places

Published as an eBook by
BookBaby (a division of Audio & Visual Labs, Inc.)
Pennsauken, New Jersey
June, 2012

Published as a mass market edition by
CreateSpace (On-Demand Publishing LLC; Amazon EU S.a.r.l.)
Charleston, South Carolina
September, 2012

This is a work of fiction. Names, characters, places, and incidents either are the product of the author's imagination or are used fictitiously. Any resemblance to actual persons, living or dead, events, or locales is entirely coincidental.

All rights reserved
Copyright (c) 2012 by Tansy Undercrypt

ISBN 978-1-623-09137-8

Published in the United States of America

This book is dedicated to:

my husband, Keith, who gave me his heart,
my dearest friend, Keith, who gave me his brain,
and my sister, Nicole, who gave me her courage.

There's no place like home.

I have lacked for nothing because of you.

Prologue

There's a kind of Bermuda Triangle here in the Midwest, an area that stretches from Unseemly Lake, Minnesota, to Endless Travails, Iowa, on to Misfortune, Wisconsin, and back again. Here, in what we've come to call the Tractor Triangle, the crops come in every year and the people appear happy enough, but the breeze off of the lake doesn't put anybody at ease and the shoppers are home and locked in tight by nightfall. The sun burns a little too brightly by day, and the long, dark shadows it casts across these small towns never seem to leave.

Everyone has a favorite story as to why the area is special (or cursed) but, in the end, it just doesn't matter which one's your favorite. What's important is why you came or why you stay. The Triangle marks its own, you see, and you're not leaving if it thinks you belong.

Drought

Mrs. Thornwit put her eyes forward and kept them forward; she could ill afford to let them fall upon little Bethany, whose moist and plump hand she clutched firmly in her own. She kept a brisk pace, at times almost dragging the girl. Beth giggled and chattered merrily away to an unseen companion and several small animals on the path.

"Mama, dress! Mama, dress *dirty!*" she squealed and pointed to the border of her walking skirt and to that of her mother's.

They were near the swamp now, the mud and decaying mulch kicked up into rough smears on the light woolen panels.

"Mama, *DRESS!*"

"It's all right, Bethany; it's all right," Alice said, squeezing her eyes shut for but a second against her perspiration and her tears. "It will be all right."

"Mama … dress!" Bethany cooed in a gleeful half-whisper, as if they were co-conspirators in a summer picnic game. They were near the edge of the water and dusk had turned to night.

They stopped and Beth followed her mother's gaze out into the water, where a dark shape was rising from the murk. Loosely the shape of a man but twice the size, it oozed across the stagnant surface towards them. When it stopped, towering over them, Alice thought she could see two darker pits that might be its eyes. She bowed her head quickly.

"S-say hello to the swamp man, Bethany," she said tersely, before her voice caught in her throat.

Gazing up, shy but curious, Beth gave the thing a tiny smile and said sweetly, "Hello, man."

Moments later, Alice Thornwit stumbled back to the main road alone, struggling to retain her composure. She clutched a lock of brown hair in her right hand, holding it away from her filthy skirt to keep it clean and safe. She would burn the clothes immediately after she reported back to Willem. And, if the harvest did not come in after the sacrifice as he had promised, she would kill him in his sleep.

Barn

I've known Conley Wilkes for over thirty years; wrote the policy on his farm off of County Road B. Not a big talker, but good company; neighborly without being up in your business. It surprised me when he called and asked for a meeting at my office on Saturday at lunchtime, imposing on both my weekend and my meal. It had to be important, so I didn't hesitate to agree, but I grumbled once or twice getting dressed to come in. It was a bright blue, cloud-free day - full sun, the perfect day to open the windows and pretend you might mow the lawn at any moment.

The door swung open precisely at noon, and the man who blocked the light across my desk wore a dark trench coat, a hat, and sunglasses. He shuddered, locking the door behind him as he turned around, out of breath as if he'd battled a September gale up the sidewalk to get in.

"Conley?" I asked, thinking this could not possibly be the man. I rose out of habit and starting coming around for a handshake.

"No! No, Reg. Please." Wilkes cringed away from me, bringing his left hand slightly up like a ward. "Just stay where you are, please, Reggie. Don't move closer and, dear God, don't touch me."

I sat back down, a shiver moving along my spine as he dragged a guest chair far away from my desk and settled into it, coat, hat, and all. His skin was incredibly pale and his cheeks were sunken. He put his hands on both of his knees and raised his head.

"I won't hurt you, Reg, but I need you to promise me that if I bolt up and outta here, you won't follow."

"Christ, Con ..." I started.

"I mean it. Let me go and do not attempt to stop me. Do not touch me for any reason."

"Okay," I agreed weakly, suddenly grateful for every drop of sunshine spilling into that room.

He moved suddenly and put a ring of keys on my desk, pushing immediately back into his seat; I jumped. Wilkes breathed very slowly and rubbed his neck, using his feet to inch the guest chair even farther away from me.

"I'm going to tell you all of it, Reg, and that will make you the only one besides me who knows. When I've finished, I'm gonna need a favor."

"Anything, Conley; you know that."

He nodded, sighed, and began to speak.

"You can tell by the smell. It's not some roadkill-no-breeze thing; it's a sharp, vinegar-type of smell, like the barn's been acid-washed on the inside. That was how I discovered it the first time. I happened to be down wind and wondered, "What the hell?"; I would've strolled right in unprotected if John Pageant hadn't stopped me with a clap on the shoulder and a hushed spill of the likely facts. We used the early afternoon to get ready and headed in around 4pm. He was a good man, John. I owe him much. I miss seeing him around town.

"I should've put the skylights and vents in after that, but money was always tight. Yes, I could've taken care of it on credit like everyone else, but I've been up to my eyeballs in debt and am too stubborn to take on more. Kicking myself today won't change the fact that, every summer, I get vampires in the barn again."

I shifted nervously in my seat. No one ever spoke directly about this stuff. I swallowed hard to put my heart back down in my chest.

"Mary and me, well, we accepted that our home was on some kind of great bloodsucker migration route. The barn is ideal for them with its high roof, deep loft, and no windows. We got the house protected well enough, but the barn gets hit every year. This is the eleventh year and the last one, too.

"I know folks say I'm an old hand at this - a natural. My God, nobody who'd ever seen one would make it sound normal let alone elegant! The first time you get a look at them, you are a changed man – and you want to scream your fool head off every single time. It's the shock of knowing you're awake and actually seeing what you're seeing. Then, the following morning, you perceive a changed order of things, you have a new understanding of what's good and what's evil, and you no longer doubt the true nature of what you used to call the food chain."

Wilkes rubbed his neck again. I prayed to every saint I could remember the name of to make him stop doing that, because it scared me in ways I couldn't even begin to explain.

"It's worse when it's someone you recognize," he continued. "It took three whiskeys for me to tell Brittany Franco's mom that I'd found her in my barn and ... taken care of it. Brittany had been missing for almost six weeks and I think everyone was hoping she'd run away from our grim little town – headed off to New York or somewheres for fame and fortune. Pretty normal for kids to think like that; heck, we all talked like that, back in the day. Mrs. Franco, she just nodded quietly at the news; made us a peach pie later in the week and attached a note about Brittany finding peace. I hope so, poor kid. I hope she did."

"Conley, you need anything? Something to drink?" I was a bundle of nerves; I needed to make him stop talking just for a moment. I gestured to the coffee pots. "I could make us ..."

He hissed at me.

I had to focus to keep my bladder under control, frantically trying to remember where I'd put the crossbow and if it was loaded. We'd never used it here, at the office, but it was comforting to have a plan. Part of you was always straining to catch the sound of something moving around up under the eaves. Damn thing was probably in the closet, where I looked longingly.

"You'd never make it there and back," Wilkes hoarsely whispered. "Please just sit very still."

We stared at each other for a little while, both of us struggling to breathe normally, then he began again.

"They're not pretty, the vampires; not like in the movies. Nothing can prepare you. Mary offers to help me every time, but I won't put her in harm's way like that, and I can't let her see them. She's a light sleeper and would probably never sleep again. You go in lookin' for Dracula and you get ... " he signed heavily. "Damn. What you get is something that will make you shit yourself blind.

"The eyes change; they get all milky except for the actual pupil. That expands. So, you get this white eyeball with a big black dot on it or, better still, maybe the pupil takes over the entire eye, making it a solid black. Least of your problems, trying to see into the windows of their souls.
"The skin is too smooth and has a moist look to it as if it would be slimy to the touch. The teeth hook out like tusks or barbs; four of

'em - two upper and two lower. When their mouths open, it's like some kind of unholy lamprey comin' atcha. The worst ..." and here he dropped his gaze to his lap, his hands in fists upon his knees, "... the worst is what happens to the neck."

I made a sound then, a mewling, lost little sound. He nodded, but didn't stop.

"When Mary was carrying our youngest, Earl, she had that thing where the bones in the hips and feet soften too much (some enzyme or whatnot) and never quite come back together the way they were. It was real painful at the time and she was self-conscious afterwards, but it was nothing to worry about. Well, the bloodsuckers have necks like that, elongated, like the spine has separated and can't line up straight anymore. The necks get maybe three times as long as usual and fold together at the back with the head floating on top.

"That will mess you up and I don't mind saying it. You go in there expecting some kind of sexy vamp slinking forward trying to seduce you and what you get is coil and recoil action with these teeth flying out at you from all directions. It's horrifying and, well, "dangerous" is the word that comes to mind, but that doesn't even begin to cover it."

I waited for him to start absentmindedly rubbing his neck, so that I could scream like a Girl Scout on a roller coaster and release some mental pressure, but he didn't.

"I go in with a shield to block and a modified pitchfork for the offensive; that's proven most effective to date, but it's not perfect, of course. For one thing, everybody keeps learning through experience; the hunter gets more focused, the hunted get more tactical. I didn't let my guard down last time; that's not how it happened." He slumped slightly at the shoulders.

"There were more in there than I estimated; five, where there are normally only two or three at most. They don't herd well, as you can imagine," Wilkes rasped dryly, intending a laugh, but offering more of a cold wheeze into the room. "I was having a tough time with one of them and didn't notice another had come up behind me. Now, I wear a neck guard and a leather coat for some armor protection, but there was nothing for it when a bloodsucker snuck up and bit me right on the ass through my jeans."

I sat, unmoving, holding my breath.

"Oh, I "won", technically. I managed to kill all of them, decapitate, and burn them. I didn't let Mary look at the bite; didn't tell her about it. Four jagged punctures in my cheek. Not good.

"I've been putting my affairs in order. Took Mary out for a real nice dinner about a week ago, while I could still eat. She's always been the light of my life. I hope she'll take the payout and get herself a nice condo in Florida – some place with full sun most of the year."

My ears perked up at the word "payout" (force of habit after a lifetime of insurance). He raised his head and sat motionless for a while. Then, very painstakingly, he reached his right hand up and removed his sunglasses, looking into my eyes directly for the first time. One eye, the right, was its normal, gunmetal blue; the other, a solid jet black.

"No! Conley!" I cried softly, but he shushed me.

"Close now. Let me finish, Reggie." He took a deep breath.

"Lately, my eyes have become sensitive and my neck aches. I was trying to stretch out a bit ago, and my jawline extended another couple of inches above my collar than where it had always been. It's time. I don't want to drag this out - have my girl see me like this. Besides, it's getting dangerous to be around her. She smells so good, like a buffet's being served beneath the skin.

"I'm going in working my same strategy this time: shield and pitchfork, axe for afterwards. At the end of it, though, I'm going to set the barn on fire and throw myself onto the thresher; I think that'll hold me in place until the deed is done."

"God," I whispered.

"When Mary comes back from town, I'm guessing the barn and the house will both be gone. But there's some new furniture waiting for her in a storage locker I rented in town. I wrote a letter that she'll find pinned to the couch. I need you to get the keys to her as quickly as you can." He gestured to the keys with his head, his one blue eye fixed on me.

"I need you to find for accidental fire and let this go. I need you to push this through, no questions asked. Tragic, but routine, you know? For me. For Mary."

I nodded. "When is this happening?"

"Today."

He rose then and, instinctively, I pulled away from him, tipping the chair back and screeching it along the waxed linoleum. Wilkes put his sunglasses on and backed slowly to the door.

"It means a lot to me - to who I used to be - that you're doing this. Mary can make a fresh start and the boys and their wives will be only too glad to help. Part of me misses them already."

"Of course," I said, masking my terror with concern.

"And ... part of me wants to eat them. It's time."

I gasped, but he didn't react to it. Conley Wilkes was through the doorway and gone. I raced to the door and flipped the deadbolt. I was nauseous; a vinegar smell hung in the room.

I put a claim form on my desk, then went to the closet to retrieve the crossbow. Fat lot of good it did in there; I'd just keep it under my desk from now on. The sun was still shining when I closed up, but I left my desk lamp on. I just couldn't bear the thought of turning out the light.

Cabin

I told them that I was taking a week off to relax at my cabin about thirty miles north of Endless Travails. I've had the place for eight years and never took so much as a long weekend there before. They don't need to know that my doctor recommended it; none of their damn business.

First, my dad, then the divorce ... I threw myself into my work. Nothing to go home for, but pretending to care for twenty hours a day chews a guy up after a while.

I lost it at some lady in the elevator two Wednesdays ago; she was wearing too much perfume and it was liquefying my eyeballs. I just started losing my shit deluxe - face hot and sweaty, spittle flying out of my mouth as I began to pound the walls and rant. She hit the emergency phone button and yelled for help. I almost clocked her for that. I'm glad I didn't, of course. Sure.

Got an escort from building security. Got a special one-on-one with my boss. Got invited to see someone, hence the doctor and his sterling recommendation. And here I am.

I drove up three days ago and I'll admit that the quiet was a little creepy at first. Okay, it's still a little creepy, but that's nature for you. There's always some rustle or scrape or thump in the woods, and then nothing but total silence.

To tell you the truth, I might drive back early. I miss the white noise and streetlight glare of the city. It's dark out here – almost too dark, if that's possible. I haven't slept with the lights on since I was a little kid, but I can't stand it all pitch black.

There's something about the dark that says it's waiting in the other room for you; it's behind the door; it's under your bed; it's pulling back the shower curtain!

God, I'm turning into a fruit bat like my mom. Nothing and no one is in the cabin with me; there's nobody watching me and, if there is, it's probably a bear who's scoping out the trash cans. RELAX. It's fine to keep the drapes closed, just don't lose it again. Must not make a habit of losing it.

I'm going to read a bit before turning in. I'll pack in the morning.

It feels a little weird to have my back to the lake, sitting on the couch in front of the picture window. Still, I've got the drapes closed, so ... whatever.

Probably not the greatest idea to bring a thriller, but I just grabbed whatever was closest to the counter at the gas station. Anything to pass a little time.

It's cold here next to the window; there must be a draft. I bet this glass hasn't been resealed in forty five years. Letting in little puffs of air almost like someone breathing. I have that prickly sensation on the back of my neck, like someone is reading over my shoulder.

OH, GOOD GOD, GET A GRIP ON YOURSELF!

I might have to make another appointment with the doc when I get home; it might be time to talk about medication or something.

This is nuts.

I just saw - or I thought I saw - movement over my right shoulder, behind the drapes on the window outside. Somebody right ... over ... my shoulder ...

Okay, there is nobody hovering in front of the window, six or more feet off of the ground. I need a drink; that's what I need. I'd kill for a scotch right now.

Is that a motor? Nice to know there are people out and about; it helps a lot. Somehow, seeing the beams from a boat's headlights bouncing up and down as it rides the waves is pretty comforting.

Damn! That is some wattage! It's almost full daylight in here, with those high beams hitting the walls. Hey, wait a minute ... boats don't have headlights ... so, where is the light coming from?

That is ... impossible. No. There's no way ... I ...

Projected on the far wall, in a silhouette created by the strange light outside, there is a head - a head and shoulders and bony hands gripping - gripping the glass near my head. Right near my head!

It's out there. Oh, my God! Something is out there and it's right behind me!

It's right over my shoulder ...

Stacks

Ingrid Henner had been a librarian for almost eleven years when her casual annoyance turned into a growing repulsion. It was odd how even the thought of them - children - had started making her flesh crawl; the noise, the smell, the overall slime of them. They were always dripping out of their noses, their mouths, or worse (she shuddered at the mental picture of toddlers picking at their diapers). It was all that she could do to keep from screaming all day every day.

It had been a stressful year and, professionally, she was barely hanging on. Those people still employed by the Randall County Public Library had to count themselves lucky (even blessed) among their fellow men. Under these conditions, the stress of keeping her Little Problem under control was tremendous. One slip, one whiff of "kid-hating librarian" on the breeze, and she could simply paint a target on her forehead and wait for HR to call. Ingrid decided to see a therapist.

It was helpful to talk. Some of the other librarians and aides didn't fit the nerdy, aloof or withdrawn stereotype, but she did. There was some wisdom in paying someone to be her sounding board - to help her draw herself out and keep it together. Ingrid made the decision to pay for her sessions in cash, thinking this was a less than opportune time to hit her mental health benefits hard. Secrets upon secrets became a way of life.

Dr. Burke was competent and gentle. The talk therapy was tremendously successful, but the exposures were not. He would accompany Ingrid to a playground or ice cream parlor where children gibbered and ran in vast numbers and they'd talk through her fears. The obsession that emerged right away was that one of the little horrors would physically touch her with their wet, snotty fingers. This preoccupation was so great that Ingrid would become paralyzed, shaking, and trying to hold back tears. After two or three unsuccessful exposures, they decided to return to weekly conversations and let the rest go for a while. Certainly, there was much to be gained by a return to the couch (for digging deeper into what was troubling her dry, tidy little life at its core).

And then Sharon Elseth didn't show.

It was Saturday, mid-morning, and the library was overrun with children waiting for a volunteer to start "Li'l Tikes' Story Hour". The readers were on a standard rotation and most of them were dependable and dedicated, but Sharon was hit-or-miss on the responsibility meter. On that particular day, she didn't arrive and didn't answer her house or cell phones. Henner was the junior staff member, so she was required to take Sharon's place. With her throat clenched and beads of sweat breaking out on her forehead, Ingrid made her way through the swarm of kids to sit on a chair at the front of the room.

"Don't look at them," she said to herself. "Don't even look up. Just read the book; stare at the words. Get through this."

Screw an hour of entertainment; she'd made up her mind to give them fifteen pages of Johnny Appleseed (with zero characterizations and no environmental sounds). In and out.

Ingrid did look up, however, to make sure that no one was close enough to reach for her, and she saw him. A little boy stood at the edge of the crowd near the back on her right. He was maybe three years old, wore a striped t-shirt and denim overalls, and had a solid booger trail from his nose to his mouth that mixed with a river of drool dripping down onto his shirt. She resisted the urge to vomit and forced her head back to the text.

"Breathe," she whispered sternly, "just breathe."

Page 15 seemed four hundred and twelve years away; she felt weak and shaky. Ingrid found she had a hard time concentrating, but no one seemed to notice; the horde of children squeaked and giggled as one huge, delirious mass. Thinking she might faint, Ingrid quickly looked up to scan the room for another adult to take over.

The little boy, that one on the right, had moved up much closer than before.

The front of his overalls were dark with drool. He wiped a damp hand across his nose, smearing God-knows-what halfway to his hairline. His eyes glittered as he grinned at Ingrid. His tongue licked his lips.

Her heart was pounding inside of her head, her hearing subsided, and the air became thick as everything moved in slow motion. She was having a hard time breathing when ... when ...

There came a rasp - a rough, moist pull on Ingrid's skin.

She looked down through the fog of panic to see that the little boy in the overalls had grasped her skirt and licked the back of her right hand.

Ingrid screamed and was immediately airborne, fleeing to the restroom before she was even aware she'd moved from the chair. She heard murmurs of faint voices, but they were far away and she couldn't make out any of the actual words. She scoured both hands in the sink until they nearly bled and then blacked out in the nearest stall for a few minutes. Ingrid's forehead was burning up and her mouth was watering, yet it was too dry to swallow. No one came to retrieve her (either out of shock or embarrassment or compassion); she stayed in the bathroom until the library was nearly silent and ready to close.
Henner's hand burned where the little monster had licked her. She forced herself to redirect her attention to anything else. Ingrid

resisted rubbing or itching it for a while, then found she'd been doing it involuntarily all along. Despondent and feeling thoroughly contaminated, she left the bathroom and approached Marilyn Fischer.

"I'm wondering," she asked with her voice trembling, "if I could close up the library for you. I need a few minutes to finish some things."

"Of course," Marilyn replied, looking at her with great tenderness mixed with a drop or two of pity. She left the building a while later, and Ingrid was alone.

Walking to the very back of the reference section, Ingrid let herself into the locked rare books room. She laid down on the cold marble, which made her feel peaceful and calm; she curled up and slept there for a long time. Normally, Ingrid felt chilled to the bone after hours and had to wear a winter cardigan to re-shelve; she woke up several hours later on the floor in just her slip, unsure when and why she'd stripped down. She wandered the deserted library, touching the books and relishing the cold. She looked down; the front of her slip was damp from drool.

"This is not happening," she whispered.

Forcing herself to dress, Ingrid locked up and went home, but could only relax long enough to pack a bag of clothes and head back to the library. She needed the darkness of the stacks, the hard chill of the stone floor. Her hand itched; it was now swollen with a faint pink line of infection winding up her arm. Ingrid felt strangely unconcerned with it. She was tired and needed to rest.

On the following night, Sunday, Henner moved her nest to the basement with the intention of never leaving, curled up behind a cabinet next to the archives. She had what seemed to be a perpetual cold; her nose ran and she was over-salivating. Ingrid casually wondered if she had a fever, because the freezing floor and walls felt like heaven. She was hungry, but just not enough to actually eat anything she could think to make or buy. The taste she most craved was salty sweet - like skin.

Ingrid Henner was excited for Monday, when the library would open again. She'd get some clothes on and go up to the main room. She could imagine a good-sized crowd at another story hour. She couldn't wait; the little children were so tender, so succulent, so delicious.

The Satanist

I pedaled into the driveway and covertly stashed my bike in the bushes off to the side. My mom would kill me if she knew. I was forbidden to come to Mrs. Belmar's house at any time, even to sell wrapping paper, seed packets, and Christmas wreaths for school. Apparently, Mom thought the old lady was "weird" and "not right" and a handful of other things that basically made her irresistible in my eight-year-old mind. Honestly, she couldn't have been more fascinating if both of my folks thought she was a superhero.

It didn't hurt that her house was haunted.

I couldn't know that for a fact without going there, of course, so I'd gone plenty of times. I'd circle the rustic Victorian home nonchalantly for a while and then creep up the alley on foot. It was amazing.

The house was big, imposing, dark and dreary - just like you need it to be if you're going to risk being grounded for trespassing. Tall, black wrought-iron gate, tattered red drapes downstairs, little round window in the attic (where you knew a face would appear if you could linger closer to sunset) - the whole deal. The best part was the abandoned carriage that sat at an angle in the back yard. Seriously, that horse-and-buggy-without-the-horse called to me in my dreams. It was right up there with finding a spaceship in someone's garage. The question instantly became not "was I going in there?", but "how am I going to get in there as quickly as humanly possible?"

I was going to ring the doorbell.

Okay, I'm a typical kid, but I'm not a brainless doofus. "You get more flies with honey than vinegar," my mom would say when I was sulking about something. I hated when she said that, but I couldn't deny that it was true. Using this, my plan was to stroll on up to Mrs. Belmar's front door and knock, introduce myself when the knock was answered, and turn on the charm deluxe.

It worked.

I had retrieved my bike, gone back around to the front of the house, strolled up the walk to the solid, castle-like door (complete with wolf's head knocker), checked for a doorbell and, not finding one, boldly knocked.

One of the curtains stirred in the front room to my right, but I couldn't see anybody. Moments later, an elderly lady in a housedress, shawl, knee-highs and fuzzy slippers opened the door. She smiled at me through enormous round glasses, which gave her eyes like an owl.

"Yes?" she asked gently.

"Hi! Hi, Mrs. Belmar. My name is Rick Metcalf. I live a couple of blocks down."

"Nice to meet you, Mr. Metcalf. How may I help you?"

"Well, I ... I don't really need help, ma'am. I was just going by and thought I'd introduce myself because I never have. Sometimes, I stop and admire your house." I gave her my Sunday School smile. That sucker never fails.

"Oh, well, that's fine - and very nice of you." She let out a little laugh and leaned out of the door as if to tell me a secret. "The house looks haunted, am I right?"

I laughed then and shrugged.

"Well, if you'd like - and if you're allowed - to come in for a snack, you're welcome to. I was just about to have something myself. That way, you could get a peek inside the house to tell your friends about." She grinned a little more broadly and took a step back in case I wanted to come in.

"Oh, I'm allowed," I lied, moving in through the doorway with zero hesitation.

She shut the door very quietly behind me and guided me on a tour through the front rooms - foyer, parlor, study, and a tiny bathroom to the left of the main staircase. It was filled with incredible stuff: a suit of armor (just like in the movies), a gazillion books, a giant rug with octopus tentacles all over it, and a stuffed boar for starters. I was speechless.

Mrs. Belmar showed me into the parlor and we sat at a small table with two chairs. She pulled a cord hanging down by the fireplace and a bell rang elsewhere in the house. Soon, I heard a slow, purposeful shuffle down the hall.

A man, probably in his late fifties or early sixties, came into the room with a tray. He had dark hair turning white and dark eyes beneath wiry eyebrows. He didn't seem surprised to find me there, and silently put down a serving bowl with two sets of plates, cups, and silverware.

"Mr. Vash has been with me for many years; I don't know what I'd do without him," Mrs. Belmar said, giving the butler a nod and a smile. "He is a mute, Mr. Metcalf, but that hardly prevents him from being excellent company." Mr. Vash nodded to her cordially and then left the room.

"Uh ... how did he know there would be two of us?" I asked her, confused.

"We don't get a lot of company here, but we are prepared for company nonetheless." She lifted the lid off of the serving dish and inhaled the steam deeply. "Marvelous," she whispered.

I peeked into the bowl to find it heaping with chunks of beef and squid in some kind of sauce. My eyes grew wide. She took a big spoon and placed a pile of the mixture on my plate. It glistened as if raw. No way I could eat that.

"Mr. Vash is a Satanist, but I don't want you to be alarmed. He's not a Satanist in a bad way," her voice chimed steadily as she served herself a portion of the food and tucked right in. "Why, when we lived in New Orleans, ..."

I don't remember the story she told me, although I left with a sense that it was the best story ever. I also left so full that I could barely stay upright on my bicycle and get home. Absolutely, I would come again, I told her. Absolutely.

That night, there were no dreams, just a feeling of sinking into nothing.

I didn't tell any of my friends that I'd gone to the Belmar house and that, by some miraculous combination of nerve and luck, I'd gotten in. Normally, I'd be tooting my own horn like a Dixieland band the next day, but I couldn't quite get there this time. Whenever the story was close to my lips, my mind would slide off of it and attach to something else; I'd lose what I was about to say. It was strange, when you consider that I was completely obsessed with the idea of going back.

I don't think three days passed before I was knocking on Mrs. Belmar's door again.

"Why, Mr. Metcalf, how delightful!" she said, giving me a warm smile. "Do come in. Once again, you're in time for a snack."

I followed her obediently into the parlor and sat down at the table. As before, the butler plodded down the hall and into the room with lunch for two. This time, when my hostess raised the lid, I spied long strips of some kind of meat and something I was sure was an eyeball in a pool of dressing.

"As I told you last time, Mr. Vash is a Satanist. He was also accused of being a cannibal when we lived in Amsterdam; can you believe it?" Mrs. Belmar giggled, shaking her head, while she served.

At that moment, yes, I could well believe it, but the story started sweeping me away from my concerns, down the Grand Canal into mysterious ports of call. It was a pleasant and satisfying lunch, and I left sleepy and stuffed as I had the first time.

All in all, there were eight lunches, eight stories about Mr. Vash, and eight dreamless nights. On the last gathering, Mrs. Belmar reached out a cool and papery hand and held mine.

"I was wondering, Mr. Metcalf, if you might want to join me for dinner on Saturday night. We'll have Mr. Vash make us something really splendid. What do you say?"

"Well ... uh ... I think that would be all right," I answered, already preoccupied with the lie I'd have to tell in order to avoid my mom's uncanny sixth sense for trouble I was about to get into.

"Oh, I'm so pleased!" she said, clapping her hands. "It's been a very long time since I've had a guest to dinner. Perhaps, afterwards, I could show you the rest of the house?"

I nodded enthusiastically; the house was immense and I'd only seen a handful of rooms. Who knew what kind of cool stuff was in the rest of it? Mrs. Belmar reassured me that I didn't have to dress up or bring anything and I was off to plot my excuse.

In the end, I learned that parents are more than willing to let their growing kids' insatiable appetites be someone else's problem for one night. After telling Mom that I'd be eating over at Brendon's, I was shoo'ed (with some barely contained glee) out of the house and into the yard with a brief reminder to use good manners.

I promised.

Sunset seemed to shrink the Belmar house, blending with its dark silhouette so completely that it seemed invisible. Only the lighted parlor stood out, the candles in the window a kind of beacon. The door opened as I pulled into the driveway; Mrs. Belmar and Mr. Vash were both there to greet me.

I was escorted, not to the parlor this time, but to the formal dining room. It was a stunning room, with big murals on the walls (of those half-goat people from mythology dancing around). The table was huge and impressive, it's heavy stone top resting on great carved legs. I almost walked into the sideboard looking up at the vaulted ceiling.

"This is really great," I said, enchanted. "No way our dining room looks like this at home."

Mrs. Belmar laughed. "Thank you, Mr. Metcalf. It really is a special place."

She steered me to my seat and Mr. Vash began to serve us from the sideboard.

"Mr. Vash painted these murals, you know. In addition to being a Satanist and a cannibal, he's an accomplished craftsman and artisan." The butler set out bread and butter and salad with dressing, some vegetables and relishes that I could not identify. He set the main serving dish on my plate.

"Mr. Vash's work is always balanced, stable - following the rule of three to its most elegant conclusion."

I was having a hard time concentrating. "Rule of three?" I asked.

"Yes, Mr. Metcalf. The world moves in repetitions of three for a total of nine; three times three is when everything comes full circle."

"Uh ...," I stammered. Mr. Vash removed the lid from the serving dish. More organ meat - this time liver and, maybe, brains. I stared at it without moving.

"Three visits per week for three weeks," Mrs. Belmar continued. "Three weekly mentions of Satan's name, three weekly servings from the sacrifice; the ninth night, an offering on the stone slab. The full moon. Full circle."

I barely heard her. There was something wrong with the meat.

"Mrs. Belmar?"

"Yes, dear?"

"There's no gravy."

Mr. Vash put his hand on my forehead and pulled my head back. Against my throat, a sweeping pressure, and all went black.

Turns out, my blood was the gravy.

The Belmar House is one hundred percent haunted. Those of us killed here linger in the basement, inside an elaborate circle Mr. Vash has drawn on the floor. We don't have bodies anymore, I don't think, because none of us feel heat or cold.

Mr. Vash comes down to the walk-in freezer every once in a while and retrieves a bag from it. It's interesting that we all thought he was a man, since we see him so clearly now. The hooves and horns are pretty hard to miss.

Mrs. Belmar never comes down and that's okay. If Vash is a lesser whatever who has to serve her, all bets are off on what the lady of the house really looks like. I just don't want to know.

We have no connection to time anymore and our memories are rapidly fading. Maybe that's good. Limbo is only torture if you remember all of your people and the crap you said you'd do. There is one thing, though, that troubles me.

I felt sad when I heard the doorbell ring yesterday.

Salt

Sylvia Ebben was in the backyard hanging wash on the lines that day, appreciating the bright colors of Spring, but acutely aware that putting the sheets out was her least favorite thing on earth. Her mind wandered while she worked, thinking about the Meals on Wheels volunteer meeting scheduled for later that afternoon.

Hearing a sound, she turned slowly; her grandmother was making her way very carefully around the corner of the house. She was wearing her favorite apron (the one with the lemons on it) and heading straight for the laundry hamper. This would not have been unusual at all, except for the fact that they'd buried her almost fourteen years before. The lemon apron had been folded carefully and tucked inside of the box with her, not to be disrespectful, but to honor who she'd been in life.

Sylvia stood motionless for a spell, gently shaking her head as if to clear it - her mouth slightly open with the shock. She didn't move until her grandmother reached out with what was left of her right hand to grab some clothespins from the basket. The shock wearing off and the truth sinking in, Mrs. Ebben screamed like a B-movie starlet and sprinted into the house as fast as her legs could carry her, spinning around to lock the deadbolt behind her once inside.

Safely barricaded inside of the house, Sylvia became aware of other screams ringing through the neighborhood. She had no clear idea of what was going on, but decided to call her friend Rose to see if she was all right and if she knew anything.

"Hu .. hullo?" Rose answered in a panicked whisper.

"Rose Beth, you are NOT going to believe what's happening over here! My stars, Rose, my grandmother is outside wrangling the wash!" Sylvia blurted out, the tension too much to contain.

Rose started to cry.

"Oh, gosh, Rose!" Sylvia responded tenderly. "Are you okay?"

"N-no. N-not okay." Rose stammered. "My uncle ..."

"Rose? What about your uncle?" Sylvia's arms broke out in gooseflesh.

"He's ... uh ... he's s-sitting on that stump in the backyard, cleaning a r-rifle from the shed."

Sylvia gasped.

Maynard Buske had been an avid sportsman and a year-round hunter. A hard, sour man on the outside, he was runny as a raw egg on the inside - prone to unstable silences, fits of irrational temper, and debilitating paranoia at the end. One day, he'd walked into Beeker's Wood with a loaded rifle and bagged himself as the trophy.

It occurred to Mrs. Ebben that these reappearing kin weren't trying to eat anybody's brains as far as she knew. They were, at least in these two cases, coming back in their old patterns of living. Her gran was a farmer's wife who got herself up at 4am to start on the chores and cooking; the fact that she'd gotten to work the second she sprang up from the ground was oddly consistent with her normal habits. Maynard, similarly, had come back to clean his guns; this was a problem.

"Now, Rose," Sylvia spoke very steadily and firmly, "I want you to stay in the house - in a closet or the pantry."

"I - I'm in my bedroom closet n-now," Rose replied softly.

"Good! Good, you just stay there, and stay away from the windows," Sylvia instructed. "Keep the phone with you, but don't leave that closet. Don't look at him, Honey. I'm going to call the pastor and I'll get back to you. "

A squeak on the porch brought Sylvia around. Her stomach knotted as she watched the front door knob turn ever-so-slightly left and then right. Grandma was trying to get in.

Eventually, she shuffled over to the rocking chair on the porch and sat down. Sylvia could see her gently moving back and forth through the sheer curtains. There were a few hairs left on her tiny head, but not much of an ear on that side closest to the window. Heaven knows where those beautiful pearl earrings got to when they couldn't hang on.

Sylvia stepped out of her shoes very carefully and padded silently into the kitchen on bare feet. She didn't really believe that the pastor was going to have the answer; she didn't think Mike Gramont could find his own backside with a map, a miner's lamp, and two assistants. Even so, she felt somehow obligated to turn to the clergy seeing as how they were dealing with matters of the living and the dead. Maybe he'd have some kind of talent for it; it certainly would be a fine time to reveal a drop of talent for something.

She called the church's main office number. The phone rang a long time and then there was the sound of the receiver being picked up and dropped on a desk or floor.

"Hello?" Sylvia yelled into the receiver. "Hello? Pastor Mike?"

A few seconds later, there came a dry, rasping sound - something between a tongue clicking and two twigs rubbing together. It occurred to Mrs. Ebben that Edna Salisbury, the church secretary, had passed on over six months ago; could it be possible that she was back on the job?

"Edna?" Sylvia whispered.

A new round of clicking and rasping ensued. Sylvia hung up quickly, suddenly breathless. She pulled the church directory out of a kitchen drawer and paged through it with her hands shaking. She called the pastor's cell phone number. Gramont answered almost right away.

"Whoever this is, you have to send someone! Send help! This is Prince of Everlasting Joy Church ..." his voice was high and tight.

"I know who this is and where you are; Mike, it's Sylvia," Mrs. Ebben interrupted. "What's going on over there?"

He squeaked, "We have a house full; we have a house full ... the church is full of 'em ..." It was clear that he would be no help at all.

"Sit tight, Mike," Sylvia sighed. "I'll figure out something."

She hung up. The Unseemly Lake Cemetery was less than a block from the church. Sylvia had a feeling that the next service would be standing room only.

"Oh, good Lord, the cemetery!" Sylvia said aloud.

That's where all of the goings on had started, obviously. Petey Witten was the caretaker out there. He lived in a tiny house at the back of the property, the last of the Old World gravediggers. He would know the most about this and, God help him, he would be the most isolated and the most overrun.

"Witten. Witten. Come on!" Sylvia's hands were still trembling as she went back to the directory a second time.

There was no picture with the entry (Petey didn't like sprucing up), but there was an address and phone. It took Sylvia two tries to successfully hit the number on the keypad. What was she going to do if he didn't answer? On the third ring, a thin and reedy voice picked up.

"Petey?" she called out enthusiastically. "Are you okay? It's Sylvia Ebben."

"Mrs. Ebben?" came the reply with a cough on the back end. "I ... I'm not feeling very good. Been real sick. Can I call you back in a couple of days?"

Sylvia thought about Edna Salisbury and felt a warm rush of gratitude that she was talking to a living person.

"Petey, listen to me. We got us ... a visitation ... right now. My grandma's on the porch, Maynard Buske is in his old backyard, and the church has filled up with its ... uh ... former faithful!"

Witten screamed and grunted as he jumped up, then screamed again. Sylvia could only imagine what he was seeing out of his cabin window. He let out a cuss word, apologized, then asked her to hold while he put the phone down and got dressed.

She heard him take a couple of deep breaths before he got back on the line.

"We're going to need a lot of salt, Mrs. Ebben. I don't have enough here or at the shed. I just checked the calendar, and the flu took me out for four days. I'm real weak and can't sow the salt myself. Can you find help?"

"Salt?" she responded, utterly confused.

"Yes, ma'am," he said. "Unseemly Lake's real ... fertile soil ... in a strange way. I learned early on to sew the ground with a little bit of salt every day to keep ... well, to keep the dead dead. But I been real sick ..." he offered apologetically.

"And now we've got company," Sylvia finished for him.

"Yes, ma'am," he said quietly.

"Don't you worry, Petey," Sylvia promised. "I can get people and I can get salt. I'll have a caravan out there in an hour or so."

Mrs. Ebben disconnected the call, holding the phone to her chest while she said a short prayer. Getting another dial tone, she activated the Meals on Wheels calling tree.

Ten people agreed to sneak out to their garages with any kind of salt they could get their hands on. Of those ten, nine actually made it to the graveyard. Ted Crowley found his father had come back and was attempting to change the oil in the Buick, so he just couldn't do it. It was understandable.

When they arrived, Petey opened the gates. Sylvia had him sit down, eat a sandwich, and drink some Gatorade. He supervised the crew while they threw salt into the open graves, tilled the ground around them, and sewed some more. Sylvia lost count of how many pounds of rock and table and kosher got used but, eventually, Petey told them it was enough and herded them into his cabin to get out of sight. The dead were trickling back onto the grounds.

It took about two hours for everyone to get back to where they'd been; there was a huge wave when the church emptied. Everything was quiet right before sunset. They restored misplaced dirt and did one last light sprinkle.

"Goodbye, Grandma," Sylvia whispered lovingly. "I'll bring you a fresh apron ... just in case."

The school nurse looked at Petey and arranged a doctor visit for the following morning. Sylvia signed him up for Meals on Wheels; heavens, he was just bare bones. Mr. Manning, the high school principal, hatched a new "apprenticeship instead of detention" scheme and came up with the names of a couple of kids who would make good candidates.

That night, the town was eerily quiet. And it was just fine.

Camera

Orson Pardo lost his only child, a girl named Pamela Jean, in 1984. She was sixteen. It destroyed his life, of course.

Pammy was crossing the street at an intersection where everyone was supposed to stop, but no one did. It was dusk and she was wearing her gray Longshoreman's Fish & Chips uniform. The brown pickup truck that paid no heed to its southbound stop sign didn't see her in the fading light; with any luck, she didn't see it, either.

Mrs. Pardo, Katja, completely lost it afterwards and was bedridden with grief. It was understandable, then lamentable, and then too embarrassing to ask about when you saw Mr. Pardo in town. She died of cancer some six years later; people speculated that it was a treatable and survivable kind, but she'd lost the will to live.

The town galvanized, mobilized, and carried out a successful crusade against reckless driving for almost a decade after Pammy's death. The city took out the four-way stop and put in a light; cops are always parked out there. The young man driving the pickup was prosecuted for involuntary manslaughter and was found guilty, but was not sent to prison; Mr. Pardo gave a very moving statement at the trial that he and his wife did not want two lives lost to the tragedy. Burton Larson (I think that was his name) received a billion community hours to serve and got out of town the very moment he was allowed.

I'm explaining all of this so that you'll know the context when I tell you about the pictures.

Pardo Photography was the only shop of its kind in Misfortune. Orson took all of the yearbook pictures, the prom photos, the wedding stills, baby snaps, and church directory shots for most of the county. His work was solid, if a little old-fashioned, but everybody loved it. Being a photographer, he had books and books of pictures of Pammy, from the obligatory baby-in-the-bathtub pose to her last Homecoming dance. Everything was catalogued - all but what was on the last roll of film that he didn't have the heart to develop.

So here we are, in the twenty-first century, and Mr. Pardo pulls up to the Buck Lake Snappy Prints to talk to me about special handling costs and entrust - at long, long last - the final roll to someone for actual processing. More than twenty years after the event itself, this is a blessing and a curse. He thinks he's ready for closure; I've seen too many people make this mistake to do anything but sigh.

"You take and we see," Orson says, nodding and putting the little black plastic canister in my hands. "We see."

"Okay, Mr. Pardo; I'll do the very best I can. I'll be extra gentle with the film," I say, almost whispering as if I'm trying not to swear over a holy relic. The whole thing makes me nervous and sad.

"Yes, yes," he says with his back to me, the front door closing quickly behind him.

"You are *so* not ready for this," I say to his shadow as it moves down the street.

Turns out, I wasn't ready, either.

We have one machine in the shop that can develop old film, but it's a slow process with a lot of human intervention required, so I decided to stay late that night and do the job myself. The lead frame crumbled, so I had to work some miracles with acetate and tape to get it to start feeding. A few hours later, I had Mr. Pardo's prints.

Well, they were and they weren't.

There were pictures of Pammy with a couple of friends, helping her mother in the garden outside, in the kitchen pretending to drink a beer - innocent and silly. Then, slightly grainier, other pictures emerged. Pammy at her senior prom (the banner behind her and her date said "Always and Forever, 1986"), in her graduation cap and gown, and carrying boxes into a building that had "Women's Dormitory" on the glass. Actual photos of what could never have happened.

The hairs stood up on the back of my neck.

Grainer still, an older Pammy got her college diploma (with her mom and dad on either side of her), then she's at a picnic with some guy who's holding her hand - the same guy she's next to in her wedding dress a frame later. In the final frame, barely viewable through the visual static, she appears to be holding a baby.

"No way," I said to myself.

I processed the film again, deciding to pull an all-nighter if I had to. Same thing; same photos, although the fragmentation of the images was increasing. The last one, the baby picture, was almost gone.

What the hell was going on? Was this some kind of a sick joke? Was this Pammy sending 'what would've been' images from The Beyond? Was it a parallel universe thing? I turned on every light in the place to help me relax. I sat very still for a long time.

In the morning, I called Mr. Pardo and told him I'd rushed his order and his pictures were ready. There was silence on the other end of the line and then a quiet "Okay." About an hour later, he came into the shop.

"Hello, Timothy. You have?" he asked pleasantly, his eyes underscored by dark circles and his hands a little shaky.

"I do, Sir, although ..."

"Although?" he stopped short, suddenly tense.

"Only three pictures were on the roll, Sir. The rest was blank."

I pushed the envelope towards him on the counter, and he opened it immediately. The friends, the garden, the beer ... all there and beautiful, but nothing else. He clutched the photos to his chest.

"Ah ...," he began, his eyes slowly closing.

"She was lovely, Mr. Pardo. I'm so very sorry for your loss. Please accept these prints as a gift from me. No charge."

He mouthed "thank you" and took out a handkerchief to wipe his eyes. I nodded, he nodded, and then he turned around and left.

I switched the shredder on and fed the other photos through.

"You so weren't ready," I mumbled as I turned it off again, "to see how good your life would've been "if only". As if you needed confirmation that the life you got has sucked."

Maybe you think I'm a jerk, but I had to call it.

Right?

Spirit House

By the time Berdene got to the post office from the hairdresser's, there was a small crowd gathered. It was a little annoying (not having any privacy for this sort of thing), but she understood how getting a package from Thailand could peak people's interest. That, and her Toby had been a good boy who was well-liked by folks in general. There'd also been a crowd on the day he'd left to become a Marine.

Lloyd Farnelle handed her the box with a little bit of ceremony and a big smile.

"I do believe this wins the record for largest number of stamps on a single box, Mrs. Wheeler!" he said, more to the group than to her directly.

She nodded; there must have been more than one hundred individual, multi-colored stamps applied to the front and down one side of the package. Berdene opened the ends first, peeling the brown mailing paper off carefully. Lloyd handed her scissors and she cut along the tape that sealed the top. Removing the straw-like packing material carefully (so as not to make a mess), she peered into the parcel for the first time.

It was a delicately carved little house.

"Oh, Mrs. Wheeler, it's a birdhouse!" exclaimed Emma Langley, delighted.

The others bent in for a peek, while Berdene fished a small card she'd spotted out of the box.

"It says "spirit house"," she read aloud to everybody.

They paused and turned to her, looking confused. Ed Smythe shrugged and handed her a note from Toby that had been tucked alongside the present.

Berdene told the group that, according to Toby's letter, spirit houses were like little shrines people had in their homes and backyards in Thailand; they were places for traveling ancestors to visit and rest while not disturbing the living.

"Well, how 'bout that?" Ed asked, letting go of the box and stepping back a little.

Emma was still peering at the little house, trying to see into the windows.

"Mrs. Wheeler, I think the inside is painted black; isn't that odd? I can't see a darn thing inside."

A couple of the others turned away from the box or nodded their congratulations to Berdene and quickly moved along.

"Sure is pretty, though," Emma continued. "Toby's very thoughtful."

"Yes, yes he is," Berdene thought to herself, closing the box, smiling at everyone, and taking her leave from the post office. She was thrilled with his kind remembrances, but she'd much rather just have him back at home.

She left the box on her dining room table overnight, not exactly sure where she'd hang the spirit house up. In the morning, there was a very faint odor permeating the room - a musty, somewhat spoiled smell.

Berdene wondered if the spirit house had been used in someone's home already; perhaps the smell was incense absorbed by the wood.

Maybe it was an antique or had been part of a temple; she could almost picture it. Marveling at how large and small the world could be at the same time, she opened the dining room window to help air the place out.

She eventually lifted the house out of its container and carried it over to a spot in the living room where the bay window cast a charming grid of light against the wall. She'd put a nail in, thinking Toby's gift would look darling right there, where everyone could see it when they came by.

Berdene was surprised by the weight of it and, had she not already known it was empty, she wouldn't have so easily dismissed the feeling of something shifting from front to back within the house as she carried it. Once on the nail, she gave it a light dusting; trying to look in the windows as Emma had done. She arrived at the same conclusion - that the inside had been painted black, but a kind of black that showed absolutely nothing. Black as pitch.

That night, she slept fitfully, convinced something was flying back and forth in front of her eyes, casting shadows onto her eyelids and causing her to put her hands up in front of her face.

In the morning, Berdene noticed that the smell had worsened. Not only that, the spirit house's black interior paint had somehow leaked onto the wall and dripped in a vein-like pattern down towards the fish tank. Grabbing some paper towels and spray, she attempted to wipe it off, only to discover that it didn't come up. It wasn't really a drip - more like something creeping through the wall itself. Staring at the house, she felt the hairs on her arms stand at attention; all of the tiny windows and the tiny door were closed.

She glanced down to take a deep breath and steady herself and noticed all four fish floating at the top of the tank, dead. All four? At once? She checked the filter and it was working fine; the water was clear and they'd had good appetites yesterday. As she wandered into the kitchen to get the net, the tiny shutter on one of the upstairs windows of the spirit house opened slowly.

Later, meeting her friend Edith Pruitt for lunch, she confessed that her new wall decoration was making her uneasy.

"I know that Toby went to a lot of trouble to ship it to me, but I think something's wrong with it, Edith," Berdene said in just above a whisper.

"What do you mean "wrong with it", Berdie?" Edith asked, unfazed.

"Well, to cut right to it, I think it arrived ... occupied."

"What on earth?" Edith asked, listening more carefully now.

"Nothing on earth, actually; that's my point, Edith," Berdene went on, keeping her voice low. "My little spirit hut has a spirit in it - and it's not a friendly one."

"Go on!" Edith encouraged, for she was a steadfast believer in This Sort of Thing.

"I've been to the library to use the computer ..." Berdene began, laying out all of the research she'd been able to gather thus far. As it turns out, spirit houses are not painted black on the inside; if they turn black, you may have a problem. Yes, they were heavily incensed (as part of a blessing), but sandalwood doesn't reek like spoiled meat; again, you could be looking at something serious if the scent of decay begins to grow.

Edith crossed herself. "You have to get rid of it, Berdie!"

"That was, obviously, my first conclusion, but listen here," Berdene continued. "Spirit houses *can* be destroyed, but shouldn't be. If you've got something angry or vengeful or just plain evil in there, burning the thing would release it to the winds to claim a greater area. The little houses, as much as they seem to be occupied voluntarily, also act as a kind of cell, confining it to a small, familiar territory."

"Heavenly days," Edith whispered.

"Or the exact opposite," her friend responded glumly. "There was no mention of the trail of ick on the wall - the smudges that wouldn't come off, but there were some passing references to unexplained deaths."

"Deaths?" Edith mouthed, barely audible.

Berdene told her about the fish - how all four perfectly healthy fish had gone belly up overnight. The paragraphs went on to say that these deaths were a way for the bad spirit to sustain itself and possibly gather power.

"What should we do, Berdene?" Edith said boldly, with resolve. Her friend was not in this alone.

"First, I need to relocate it to an outside spot to test these theories for one more day. Things are happening quickly, so I don't think I'll need more than that. Then, if I'm not wrong, I'll need some help."

"Anything," Edith said, taking her hand. "Anything you need, me and Karl are here for you."

Berdene left the diner feeling better than when she'd arrived; better, but not safer. She stopped into the music store before going home and bought some sandalwood incense and a holder. The young man at the register smiled at her purchases and said she was in for some "excellent mojo". Whatever that meant, she hoped so; seemed like a good thing.

Once home, she avoided looking at the spirit house directly, quickly setting up the incense holder on the counter between the kitchen and the dining room. She lit the first stick and felt a little less tense. It was a pleasant scent, if a little heavy. Still, she welcomed the "mojo" it could bring.

"Bless this house," Berdene said softly.

She kept moving, going straight out of the back door to the elm in the corner of the yard. It had fallen sickly almost a season before, but she'd tried her best to save it with various treatments that hadn't brought it around. Berdene was almost certain that hanging the spirit house here would kill it, so she apologized and asked for its help. She retrieved the hammer and a nail out of the garage and drove it in.

Back inside, she slipped on her quilted oven mitts and swallowed hard.

"Just tear off the Band-Aid, Berdene; grab it and go," she told herself firmly.

She walked purposefully over to the spirit house, took it off of the wall in one motion, turned and strode out of the open back door to the elm, and hung it up. She was trembling all over. Halfway down the main hallway, all of the windows and the door had opened on their own.

Once back inside, having locked the door and thrown the oven mitts away, she felt instantly lighter. She resisted the temptation to look out in the yard at the house and, instead, strolled up to the kitchen counter to keep the incense going. She would move the burner into the bedroom with her when she turned in; maybe she'd actually sleep tonight.

Around midnight, still not sleeping, Berdene heard what she could only describe as a little wooden door opening and closing repeatedly - being slammed, actually. A bit of wind picked up, throwing leaves and sticks against her window. More than a handful of times, the garage motion sensor floodlight went on, filling the room. On towards three or four in the morning, she got up to look at the light to see what had triggered it; along the fence, the black shadow of the hut stretched towards the main house. To her horror, Berdene found that the shadow wasn't a large rectangle with a pointed roof, but a squirming thing, lashing out with tentacles and horns. It couldn't quite reach and she reacted instinctively, picking up a lipstick from her dressing table and drawing a cross on her windows.

"You just stay where you are, devil," she whispered.

She lit more incense and laid back down, nodding off until morning.

Once up, she dressed for battle, putting on what she jokingly called her "farm britches", a pair of tough denims and a long-sleeved shirt. As she rolled up the sleeves, she remembered that the shirt had originally been Paul's; she suffered a wave of missing him and then went downstairs, bringing the incense holder and sticks with her, lighting more in the kitchen. No sense taking chances.

After coffee and toast, Berdene put on her boots and went out into the backyard. Tears stung her eyes as she surveyed the area. The elm was blackened, as if it had been burnt, and two doves lay dead on the ground under the spirit house. It was silent out there; no birds, no squirrels, and no bugs. The morning glories on that side of the fence hadn't opened; most of the flowers were twisted and dead on the vine.

"We're almost done, you little bastard," Berdene thought to herself. She knew better than to speak directly to it and wasn't anywhere near stupid enough to issue a challenge. Instead, she stepped back inside for a moment, put some sandalwood ash on her neck and wrists like perfume, grabbed her purse, and got her keys. She called Edith and Karl's house as soon as she was more than a block away.

"I don't mind telling you, Berdie, that this whole story is a little crazy," Karl confided, handing her a mug.

She took it gladly. "Yep, crazy with a capital "K" and one hundred percent true."

Edith joined them at the table. "How were things last night and this morning?"

Berdene told them everything - the wind, the shadow, the burnt bark, the dead doves, the horrible silence. They sat motionless while she recounted everything and then they collectively sighed.

"Damn," Karl said after a long period of quiet. "What do we do?"

"While the spirit house shouldn't be burnt, it can be buried," Berdene began. "Saying that, I don't want to contaminate the ground with it. I was thinking of some place where it can do no harm, or maybe even do some good."

"I don't follow," Karl said, looking confused.

"I do," Edith interjected, nodding. "Sewers."

"That's right," Berdene nodded and smiled. "Install it at the end of the line; let it kill the occasional rat or cockroach, but keep it in the dark away from what's good in this town. Let it lie in a pool of filth forever."

Karl whistled and wiped his brow. "You ladies don't mess around. When do we need to act?"

"Right now," Berdene said gravely.

"Okay," Karl said, getting up. "I'll get the truck and take care of it."

"No," Berdene corrected him, "not alone you won't. I need to come with you; that spirit's current grievance is with me."

"WE will come with you," Edith corrected further. "I'm not just sitting here by myself; we are in this together."

Karl sighed and got his keys.

Within ten minutes, the navy blue van marked with "Karl's Pest Control (call us when vermin have you squirmin')" in white letters pulled into Berdene's driveway. They all got out of the cab carefully, and Karl pulled his prize trap from the back. It was a stainless steel wolverine trap, solid and heavy. He'd never used it before and had wondered if he'd ever get the chance. "Be careful what you wish for," he thought with a smirk.

The silence was palpable in the backyard. Edith gasped and held a hand to her throat when she saw the doves. Karl flipped down his metal faceplate and pulled on his leather and chainmail gloves. He opened the trap, pulled the spirit house off of the tree, put it into the container, and bolted the lid shut. He did not make a face or a sound when he felt something shift within the little house and start to struggle against him. He didn't think the situation could be helped by screaming.

The trio drove out to the end of the asphalt on the almost forgotten County Road 11. There, Karl used a special plate-lifter to bring up what was the farthest manhole cover from town. He climbed down into the blackness on a bent and rusted service ladder, carrying a flashlight. Within moments, he'd returned to the van, pulled out a length of screen, a mallet, and four small spikes. He instructed Berdene to hand him the stuff as soon as he called out for it; Edith stood stiffly by her side.

He got the trap from the van, opened it, grabbed the spirit house by its roof, and moved quickly back down the latter.

"Screen!" he barked suddenly.

Berdene handed it down.

"First spike!" he called out next.

Edith was ready with that one. There came a sound of metal being hammered into concrete, a sound that was repeated three more times.

When he emerged from the hole, Karl was pale and feeling nauseous. They urged him to rest, but he put the cover back on and secured it before sitting down.

"Put it in an alcove on its back, like a coffin," he said slowly, getting his breath. "Put a screen over the alcove and spiked that down."

Both Berdene and Edith looked relieved.

"Damnedest thing, though," he continued, his color improving. "By the time I was done driving the spikes in, there was a dead rat floating at my feet. Little asshole is going to put me out of business!"

They started laughing then, and drove away smiling.

Later that night, after a celebration of hot wings and beer at the bowling alley, Berdene wrote to Toby at his station address. She told him that she appreciated his amazing generosity and hoped he knew how much staying in touch meant to her, but she didn't want him going out of his way to send gifts anymore. All she needed, she wrote in capital letters, was the occasional postcard and for him to come home safe.

Old Clothes

We had these scarecrows in the side yards, a small grove of trees apart. Well, they weren't scarecrows yet, more like wooden crosses the size of a man waiting for some old clothes. Mom didn't feel like digging around in the attic; she gave us five dollars and told us to ride into town to the thrift shop and pick up something to flesh them out, so that's what we did.

In the far corner of the store, we found an old black tuxedo, frayed and partially eaten by moths. Next to it, a wedding dress, stained, with the lace overlay practically shredded. We thought it would be a hoot to dress the scarecrows as man and wife, and there was no way Pearl could've sold these, damaged as they were. We got it all for a dollar and celebrated our luck by getting some ice cream down the street.

Now, Mom pretty much rolled her eyes at everything we did, my twin brother and me, and this was no exception. I say that, but I believe she actually thought it was clever. Eyeing a smear of something chocolate on my shirt, she didn't say anything - just held out her hand for the change. We were tasked with putting the suit and dress on the forms, so we did that and then wandered off to find trouble elsewhere.

The next morning, we crawled out of our bunk beds and opened the window; the first bright light of day was spreading across the yard and fields. It was going to be a hot one. It was Sherm who called it out - said the tuxedo scarecrow didn't look right, and we strained our eyes. Sure enough, it was at the edge of the plot and not in the middle of the thing where we'd originally staked it. I immediately thought Sherm had snuck out and moved it, so I punched him hard in the arm and we wrestled before Mom told us to knock it off and come down for breakfast.

I noticed, while getting dressed, that the bride was moving a little bit, the torn pieces of lace lifted up and out by the wind. It reminded me of a girl twirling slowly in front of a mirror. Weird. No breeze that day.

I put the groom back where he was supposed to be and then Sherm and I rode our bikes down to the creek to see if we could catch some bullheads. Those were long, beautifully bright days and they went like lightning. Before you blinked, the sun was setting and the first of the bats were flitting from one tree to the next. We headed back towards the house at top speed, passing the groom, who was now out of the field and a few feet down the path to the house. We passed it in silence, wondering what the heck was going on there. In the way kids do, we just dismissed it; it was suppertime and we were too hungry to care.

Dad busted our chops for screwing around with the scarecrows, and told us to put them back tomorrow and leave them alone. Our protests did nothing, so we just sulked and ate. Mom went to the window frequently, a little agitated. That's how she got when a storm was coming, so I wondered if we were in for a doozy.

It was my turn to help Mom with the dishes, so I started stacking the plates. She was at the window, silent as a mouse, and staring intently. I walked over and stood next to her, looking out. A chill passed through me and I think I made a sound. The bride was standing in the corner of her field nearest to the bike path and the groom was halfway down it now, well on his way to her.

Mom put her arm around my shoulders. "They're moving towards each other. Been doing that all day. You can't see them do it, though; it happens the moment you turn your head."

"What's going to happen when he gets to her?" I asked in a whisper.

"I have no idea," she replied carefully, "but you boys are not to go out into the yard for any reason tonight, Louis Michael, or I will get the belt."

I nodded. No need to doubt a threat like that. We cleaned up in silence, obsessed with peeking out of the windows.

None of us successfully watched television that night; our eyes sought the windows frequently, even though we couldn't see anything at that angle in the pressing dark. When I told Sherm, he had just whistled, not doubting any of it for a second. He was not a gullible kid; he knew the difference between goofing around and dead serious at the cellular level, especially when it came to me (a "twins" thing, I suppose). Dad had been a harder sell until he saw whatever it was for himself. We heard him say, "Damn!" a couple of times from the kitchen and had looked at each other knowingly.

At 9:30pm, after however many hours of pretending to be a normal family with normal scarecrows, my mom shushed us all and shut out the lights, motioning us to the sliding glass door and urging stealth. When all of us were arranged so that we could see, she pointed out to the yard. The groom had reached his bride, and both were circling each other in plain sight.

It was like an invisible tornado was forming around them as, joined at the base, the wooden forms began to spin together faster and faster. The groom's vest and jacket opened up; the bride's substantial skirt fell away; the tuxedo pants began to shred in the unseen wind, pulling against where we'd pinned them to the coat, and sliding down; the row of tiny buttons and loops on the bride's dress started coming apart from the collar to the waist.

"Uh ...," said my dad in a soft and suddenly uncomfortable voice.

"Oh, my stars," my mom replied, tightening her grip on Sherm and I.

The groom, recognizable by only a very few tatters of black material still clinging to his wooden beams, now thrust himself onto the bride form (who was down to a layer of netting and part of a sleeve). They started to ... uh, well, they started to ...

"Oh, hell!" Dad yelled, clamping a hand over our eyes and leading us away from the window at the same time. We complained and tried to get out from under the vice-like grip, but didn't have a prayer.

We heard Mom open the sliding door and yell, "Hey! Hey, cut that out!" into the yard, but she came back inside just as quickly and started pulling the blinds down over all of the windows along the back of the house. Dad let us go when she headed upstairs.

"Now, boys, you're going to bring your sleeping bags into our room tonight and sleep on the floor like we were camping. You will not look out of the window - any window - for any reason until I say so. Understood?"

We looked at each other and looked back at him shrugging, acting casual. We were, of course, desperate to get to the first available window and stare out of it immediately, risks of punishment be damned. Dad's eyes narrowed.

"Actually," he said flatly, "I think it would be fun to sleep on the floor with you tonight."

Inwardly, we groaned.

The night passed with all of us pretending to sleep, pretending not to hear the sounds of sticks smacking together in the vegetable garden just outside. As dawn came, my mom got out of bed, dressed, went downstairs, and then out the back door into the yard. There was the sound of her getting wood from the pile under the deck and the woosh of a fire starting in the dirt pit.

She moved about then, picking up bits of clothing and fabric, then set to the wooden crosses themselves; she might've pulled the beams apart with her bare hands.

I heard her murmur, "I'm sorry, but I have young children in the house" and then the fire began to crackle and pop a little under its new burden.

We were allowed to get up when everything was over and done. Dad let Sherm and I help make two more scarecrow forms in the garage, but sent us up to the attic to look for clothes. We stuck to a basic plaid shirt-and-overalls fashion statement this time, desperately wishing that the "guys" would want to play cards together or something and the whole business would start again.

Blue

Blue ran and, as he did, he felt every single one of his eleven years strain at him - screaming, burning away. He was an old dog and moving at top flight speed was not required of him anymore. Even so, he headed into the trees towards the pond as fast as he could go.

When Mrs. Bergman had dropped to all fours next to the dining table at the dessert course, the others thought she was having a seizure. Blue and Paco, however, knew differently. She was changing - becoming something else, something dangerous.

The werewolf rose with its head low, beginning to move in a confident half-circle around the children. Blue knew he couldn't get this wrong; Mrs. Bergman would kill them all. He streaked low on her blind side, coming from the corner of the room, sinking his teeth deep into her haunches on the right, bruising the tendon by the knee at the very least. She howled, turned on a dime, and slashed him across the chest as she went down and struggled up again. Bleeding now, he corrected his course and dove through the doggy door.

"Please don't let me mess this up," he thought as he flung himself down the front porch steps. "Please ..." If she didn't follow, all was lost.

Blue need not have worried. At one one thousand, two one thousand, three one thousand, four ... the front door exploded.

He could hear Paco barking his insane Chihuahua yip-yip-yip and wished he would stop. "Don't distract her, buddy; I have to get us into the woods." His eyes stung; the full moon made navigation a little easier, but the cataracts took away any other advantage. Blue used memory to zig and zag through the brush and dead tree stumps on his way to the water. He could hear bushes split, underbrush snap, and logs thump as the werewolf flew after him. It was not an even fight.

He could see the edge of the pond and the bright outline of the dock stretching into it. He allowed his heart to hope some, as his left forepaw got tangled in a dried mass of vine and his body was thrown head over tail for six feet or more. Blue shook his head, tried to focus.

Blazing yellow eyes approached slowly; Mrs. Bergman had arrived.

She lunged at him, biting him at the top of the shoulder near the neck, playing with him. The wolf would kill him when it had made him suffer just a bit.

Blue closed his eyes. Why was he so sleepy?

A familiar yip-yip-yip sounded twenty yards away. Blue looked out to see Paco jumping up and down excitedly on the rough sand beach, running in tiny circles, wagging his tail.

He tried to bark - tried to warn him about the werewolf, but could only gather enough air in his throat for a wuffle. Sensing she had already won this round, but greedy for extra cruelty, she kicked dirt up over the injured Heeler and bounded off towards the sound.

Blue wuffled again, turning his head painfully to watch his little friend bound onto the dock, jumping playfully from board to board, with his tail still wagging. The werewolf went insane at the display, launching onto the dock full tilt. The planks were damp and slippery from a late afternoon rain; she began to tumble onto her backside, spinning closer to the edge.

The Chihuahua offered her a delicate and affirming, "Yip!" as he leapt into the water with a small splash and began to swiftly paddle.

Mrs. Bergman, roaring in panic, careened off of the end of the dock into deeper water. Flailing and howling, the werewolf grabbed one of the wooden posts and clawed at it in an attempt to gain a foothold and climb. It turned to mulch in her paws. Disintegrating, two sections of the dock came down onto her head just above the right eye with a dull thwack. The wolf went down below the surface of the water, popping up in a minute or two a little father out in the waves, completely motionless.

"Interesting," Blue thought surveying the scene. Wolves can swim all right, but Mrs. Bergman had always been terrified of water. His hunch had paid off.

Paco shook himself off and ran over to the older dog, leaning up against him in a hard ball, which caused Blue significant pain. Before he drifted off to sleep, Blue realized that the little dog was applying what pressure he could to stop the bleeding.

That's where their family found them, the men bringing a net and hooked poles from the shed to retrieve Mrs. Bergman's body from the water. She had changed back when they reeled her in at last.

Both dogs were honored as heroes; Paco got his celebration right away, and Blue got his when he'd returned home from the veterinary hospital. There was a steak and a sweet potato with a dab of honey and some kind of dog-friendly ice cream; wonderful, if not exactly perfect.

Mr. Bergman disappeared in the commotion following his wife's transformation and enraged exit from the house that fateful night. His car remained in the driveway, however, so it appeared he'd successfully escaped on foot to avoid questioning.

"On paw is more likely," Blue confided to Paco, who nodded. Every now and then, when they went into the yard to do their business, both had the unshakable feeling that they were being watched.

Mr. Nightmare

I have to concentrate. Man, I could fall asleep right here, standing up.

I need to pull it together. Get it together.

I miss my nine-to-five (and I never thought I'd say that and actually mean it). Sure, it was a grind, but it was *one* grind - just one. Now, life is grinding away to the tune of three part-time jobs and I am losing my mind here.

I hardly sleep anymore. I joined the recession's walking dead about three months ago, six weeks after my unemployment benefits ran out. Still, I consider myself one lucky zombie. I'm not kidding! I'm grateful to be scraping by, I just wish that I could sleep. It doesn't help that I've been having the same nightmares I had when I was a kid. No joke. What's surreal is that they're just as scary now. Seriously. I wake up soaked in sweat.

There's this one "monster man" that I used to dream about repeatedly; I called him "Mr. Nightmare". He always wore a big, black trench coat and had a black, broad-brimmed hat pulled way down over his face (so that all you could see was the smile). God, the smile! Thick, greenish black lips pulling away from an impossible number of sharp, yellow teeth stretching across his face from one cheekbone to the other. He .. it ... would reach out towards me and the arm would push out of the coat sleeves revealing two twisted, clawed fingers on each end. Black, pointed talons for nails - dull and jagged. Jesus, those finger prong things would start reaching out with that grin in the background and I'd wake up screaming loud enough to shake the whole house.

I've wondered if I wake up screaming now. I can't tell, but at least none of my neighbors have complained.

Okay. Concentrate. It's retail carnage at America's favorite megamart; there must be forty gazillion people here and they're all buying toilet paper. I don't know why I notice stuff like that, but - hey - whatever it takes to stay in the game – to stay *alert*. Today's a double shift. A double shift complete with angry mob, well prepared to shit themselves if the economy gets any worse. I'm here for you people.

I barely even look up any more, it's just greet, scan, bag, change, repeat. Repeat until you're in your kitchen making a sandwich for dinner and you can't remember driving home for the life of you. It's like being in a fog.

Concentrate.

Somebody stood in line to buy gum? You gotta be kidding me! Did you eat a garlic bulb for lunch, Sir? Is this a halitosis emergen-

Wait. *Wait.*

No.

I greeted, scanned, bagged ... no. The hands pushing the money over to me are ... two twisted, clawed fingers at the end of a black sleeve.

Get a grip!

This is NOT REAL.

I'm looking away. Good. I'm looking back ... looking back ...

Oh, my God, two twisted, clawed ... still there. I can't look up.

I don't have to. My peripheral vision gives me a big, black silhouette - a man in a hat. I feel sick ... sweaty.
He's leaning in. I can almost see the curve of the lips and the teeth -

the yellow teeth lining up from one side of the head to the other.

Wake up!

WAKE UP! I've got to be sleeping! I hear someone call out at the back of the line "Is there a problem?"

YES! Yes, there's a fucking problem! Can't they see it? Why don't they see it?

Two sets of claws push the money even closer to me across the counter. If it keeps leaning in like that, it's going to touch me. I need to get out of here.

I think the fire alarm just went off.

Wait.

No.

That's me.

I'm screaming.

Green

Robbie Helm was an idiot. Not the kind of idiot you could feel sorry for, mind you, or even get inspired by because he'd somehow accomplished great things. Nope. Helm was humanity's lowest common denominator going nowhere fast, but he was doing it with a fully stocked bar.

Working at the flour mill was the town's default employment option, and most of us took it. Having something fairly dependable frequently allowed us to be irresponsible, and balance the *pro* of actually having a job with the *con* of nights spent in every local den of iniquity we could find.

It was Helm, me, and a weasily little add-on named Strogsfeld that formed a well-known troubled trio staggering down Main Street most nights. Strogsfeld was the last to rack up his fourth DUI, meaning the three of us had nothing in the way of transport except feet. This brings us back to Robbie's stash.

It was St. Patrick's Day and Helm was not about to pass the time in quiet reflection at the trailer park. We were summoned to his digs about 5pm, his slurred command to "'get our asses right over there" providing us a much needed plan for the night as well as confirming his plan had started without us.

"Hey, fookers!" Robbie called from the doorway of his hovel, his six foot bulk filling the opening completely. His reddish hair was freshly crewcut and his face was flushed pink with sun and the sauce. He was wearing a ridiculous emerald green shirt with a leprechaun or something on it. Idiot.

"We are gonna die of alcohol poisoning tonight, man," Strogsfeld muttered under his breath.

"Heh," I responded, thinking on some level that it was a real possibility.

"Come an' haf a drink with me, fellas! Welcome to the palace!" Helm made a sweeping grand gesture with a fifth of whatever he was holding at the time and spun himself off-kilter, stumbling back into the dark room where we heard a solid 'thud'.

"Deep breath," I said to Strogsfeld, who took a gulp of fresh air and held it fast as we passed over the threshold.

Robbie was not in danger of being called a "neat freak" any time soon and, between the many-moons-unvacuumed carpet, the bags of garbage in the kitchen that never quite made it out to the curb, and the pervasive stench of mildewed jockstrap, it was always ripe in there - "stockyards in July" ripe.

"Jeeeeeeesus," Strogsfeld said, getting his first big whiff and spying the bar at the same time.

Helm had filled a wall unit with booze, from floor to ceiling. For a thick lug you'd never immediately describe as "nimble", he had a surprisingly elegant way of picking up a bottle of something at the store and coming home with two more deftly tucked into his jacket and his pants. It was kind of a thing of beauty, if you glossed over the theft part.

"Pick wot ya want, boys!" Helm called out while he struggled up out of the couch where he had landed. "No glasses, 'course, an' no ice neither."

"Why get fancy, right?" I said, giving him a smile and picking out a bottle of firewater for myself.

"TOO RIGHT, brutha!" he boomed, grabbing up a piece of newspaper from a huge pile next to the television. "Got somethin' special tonight, kids!"

Strogsfeld and I had settled on the couch, screwed the caps off of our bottles, and toasted our host's good health. He smacked an advertisement down in front of us on what was probably the coffee table under all of that glossy porn.

"Yessir, fookers! We got us a dancer!" Robbie righted himself and began to gyrate. Needing a distraction urgently, I grabbed the ad and began to read.

"Girls for every occasion! Unforgettable beauties; exotic dancing; one of a kind entertainment! Book now!" I whistled between my teeth. "Dude, I don't know."

"What don't you know?" Helm stopped flailing about and looked at me.

"Well," I hesitated. "A stripper? How are we gonna pay for that? And how do we know her mack daddy doesn't come with and waste us all for your stash?"

"Mack daddy?" Strogsfeld asked me, grinning like he'd caught me singing love songs in the shower. I ignored him.

"Her handler, protector, whatever!" I shook my head, looking at the two men.

"No worries, bro'!" Robbie said with a smile, beginning to gyrate again. "I ordered us somebody for 7pm, and I mentioned that I wanted somebody hungry for tips. You guys can pay me back." Strogsfeld snorted and took another drink. I groaned.

"7pm? That's only two hours! This place is a hellhole, Dude!" I said, pointing to the various piles of debris everywhere.

"Right! Crap!" Helm stammered. "I better get some clean sheets on the bed! Make it easier to ... TAKE THE HELM!" He whooped and shrieked like a crazy man and we all laughed. It was an old line and getting older.

"Seriously, Helm," I began.

"Shut it, Dodd," he suddenly rounded. "I'm havin' me some fun tonight and you can sit out here an' chaperone for all I care. Got it? I hope your chronic case of tight ass isn't contagious." He looked defiantly at Strogsfeld.

"I'm in," Strogsfeld said with a nod.

"Okay, okay," I admitted defeat with a hands up gesture. "Exotic dancer, check."

I was nervous then, more nervous than I could justify, so I put the girlie mags into a loose pile and shoved them under the recliner. I couldn't do much about the smell, but I could keep our lack of class from assailing her eyes as well as her nose. Robbie went into the back bedroom and did ... whatever he did.

I began to drink in earnest and my discomfort grew.

At 6:55pm, there came a knock at the door and we all jumped. No sound of a car pulling up or anything, just that knock. A creepy smile spread across Helm's face as he whispered, "Jackpot! She must live at the park!" A couple of fist pumps later, he was opening the door and there she was.

Our entertainment for the evening was tall (maybe 5'10") and willowy; long dark hair, dark eyes, and dark red lips. She was wearing a gold harness type thing that made her breasts pop out and green sequin shamrocks glued to her nipples. A gold g-string was barely hanging on farther down and she kicked off delicate golden sandals before we could warn her about Robbie's health hazard of a carpet. She was striking, but not for her features in general (although they were great). She was striking because, well, she was green.

Head to toe. Every inch of visible skin. Green. A slightly darker shade than emerald green had been sprayed on her - even the insides of her hands and the soles of her feet. It was the most incredible body paint job ever done, and I couldn't help but stare.

Helm was actually trying to be charming and gentlemanly, offering her a beverage and pointing out the location of the bathroom if she needed it. She didn't talk, just smiled at all of us, opening her purse and pulling out a CD she turned over to him. He fumbled with the thing for a couple of moments, then put it in the player and pressed "start", resuming his seat on the couch with us.

The music started, a grinding, slow, horn-heavy jazz piece that almost disguised Strogsfeld's rhythmic panting.

"This is better than Star Trek," he muttered, his eyes half-closed.

Robbie was silent.

I was still trying to find even a millimeter of skin on her body that remained white or tan or black - any fleck that had been missed. I needed to find it and I couldn't tell you why.

The jazz piece finished and Helm started whooping like a madman, clapping and yelling like he was at a concert in the nosebleed section. Strogsfeld and I also applauded, seeming weak and restrained next to Robbie's outburst. He didn't even notice. She motioned to Helm to move over to his easy chair and the next song started.

An edge this time; hard drops and stops made for a lap dance that would've convinced my grandmother to cut me out of her will had she known I'd watched. Robbie's eyes were bugging out and he was bright red in the face, like he was holding his breath.

"Great goddamn," whispered Strogsfeld, who took a long draw from his bottle and shook his head.

Somewhere in the middle of the dance, putting her rear end right up in Helm's face, she looked at me. I swallowed hard. Her lips were smiling, but her eyes weren't. So dark. I didn't see a pupil. I looked away quickly.

Helm completely losing it again marked the end of that song and Strogsfeld took his place in the chair. Robbie kept smacking me going, "Yeah, man! YEAH!" and pounding the couch with his fists. I kept my bottle to my lips, wanting it to be over. I didn't want a lap dance; I wanted to go home. Drink. Drink.

On the one hand, Strogsfeld's rave number seemed to go on forever; on the other hand, it seemed to last only thirty seconds or so, and then it was my turn. I shook my head, "I'm good; thanks," I said.

"Don't be a homo," Helms growled.

"TOTALLY better than Star Trek," Strogsfeld added with a dizzy grin.

"No, I'm ... good. Really. So drunk ..." I began, hopeful.

Robbie stood up, grabbed the front of my shirt, dragged me out of my spot (bottle and all) and basically flung me into the recliner. I was stunned. The dancer just smiled and struck a pose. The music started.

Weird, popping electronica. Good bass. She began to shimmy strategically, shoving herself practically on top of me and then pulling away. I tried to concentrate solely on the music - distract myself, but I was more distracted by her smell.

Was it the body paint that gave off that very faint acetic smell mixed with some kind of sweet perfume? It was like finding an old bottle of apple cider vinegar in the pantry.

She got right in my face at one point, nose to nose, and I tried to pull back, but there was nowhere for my head to go. Bright red, smiling lips. Same dead, black eyes. I controlled the urge to shudder.

When the music ended, I thanked her and grinned to my compatriots as expected (like a lunatic) and rushed back to my original spot.

Helm had sprung up and gently escorted the dancer over to the stereo while he fished out her CD from the changer. He was whispering into her ear, in heavy negotiations. I saw her look at all of us, smile, and nod. He gestured down the hall, and she gave us another look before picking up her purse and heading towards the bedroom.

Arms up and legs pumping in a pose of sporting triumph, Helm dug his wallet out of his pants and pulled out a hundred dollar bill.

"Getting the full meal deal, gentlemen," he whispered excitedly. "Don't wait up."

He bounded off down the hallway, entered the bedroom, and shut the door.

"Jesus Christ," I said, half sick.

"Best St. Patrick's Day ever!" Strogsfeld agreed.

We started hearing muffled shrieks and thumps almost immediately, so we turned on the television and jacked up the volume as high as it would go.

An hour passed, maybe a little more. Things had gotten quiet in the back room. Almost on cue, the bedroom door opened, flooding the little hallway with light. The dancer took maybe a half-step out of the doorway and gestured to us. The harness and the g-string were no longer included in her silhouette. My heart started racing.

"No," I whispered, reaching out a hand to restrain Strogsfeld, but he was already gone.

"A threesome?" I heard him say. "Best party *ever*."

He moved down the hall, looking back over his shoulder at me and grinning.

"Keep that volume up, man," he said before she wrapped her arms around him and pulled him into the room.

I did. I kept the volume up. And I kept fantasizing about leaving the trailer, held in place only from the threat of how Helm would treat me going forward. Things would get rough down at the mill if I bailed but, oh God, I wanted to bail.

I watched a movie on cable, then I started watching another.

At the three-hour mark, I woke from dozing and heard nothing from the back bedroom. I started wondering if the rest of the party had passed out and got instantly pissed. I could've gone home hours ago. Idiots.

The door to the bedroom was open a crack, but there was no one in the hall beckoning me to sin. I didn't know what to do; leave a note? Head out? Helm had paid the girl, right? Oh, fuck, was I on the hook if he hadn't? I would wake his ass up with a baseball bat if he thought of sticking me with that! Adrenaline took over my common sense. I got up off of the couch and walked purposefully down the hall.

There was a smell. That vinegar smell, mixed with something else thick and cloying. I almost gagged. "Helm probably has a plate of ramen noodles under his bed from 1994 for starters," I told myself, trying to prevent the stench from registering. "Pay the dancer; I'm going home," was the message, no matter what I saw in there. Easy in, easy out.

I pushed the door open gently, not wanting to disturb her if she'd fallen asleep. I saw a hand at the bottom of the door; someone had fallen asleep on the floor. It wasn't Robbie's plate-sized paw, so I nudged a little harder to get Strogsfeld up. The hand rolled away from the door and out into view on the carpet. It wasn't attached to anyone.

I stepped away into the hall pushing against the door; it opened wide at the very instant I fell back.

The single lamp on the nightstand cast its minimal forty watts on what was left of both men. Pieces and parts. So much blood.

From between the bodies, the dancer uncoiled, her lips in a familiar smile. This time, the smile kept spreading until she revealed a mouthful of sharp, pointed teeth - a trail of dried blood down her chin and her chest. Her fake forehead had come loose in the fray and rolled up to reveal two more pairs of black eyes stacked on top of the others. From her backside, something flexed and extended; not a vestigial tail, more like a tentacle with a barb at the end. She flicked it at me and playfully hit the door.

"Oh, my God," I gagged and turned to run. I could hear the sheets crinkle as whatever that was moved from the bed. "No ..."

It was not a long way to the front door, but I was only halfway to the outside world when something hit my back with the force of a log being thrown, and I was down.

The tentacle wound around my chest from shoulder to shoulder, pinning my arms down and turning me over. The creature moved on top of me on all fours with its face only inches from my face. The lower jaw opened to allow an impossibly red forked tongue to leave all of those cerated teeth behind and lick me up one cheek to my hairline. I screamed behind lips I held shut. There was a rasping sound - laughter? - from her as I squinted my eyes shut and she pried open one of them with her fingers. She moved her head so that her six black eyes could take turns looking into my one watery blue one. I was so dead.

"Not from around here, are you?" I mumbled. Might as well go out acting clever.

That rasping again, obviously laughter this time, and the tentacle's grip loosened very slightly. She sat up and released a belch that would've won a contest in college, distractedly rubbing her belly. Another belch brought a slightly troubled look to the face; the lips frowned and the eyes darted around. The tentacle released me, but patted my chest as she got up and moved to the bathroom door.

I started crab-walking backwards, my eyes on her as she looked back at me before going in. She shrugged, holding her gut, and smiling slightly. She closed the bathroom door behind her. I scrambled up to standing and ran like hell.

I've been running ever since. I'm wanted for the murders of Robert Helm and Scott Strogsfeld, of course - irony being the constant companion of the innocent. I'm also acutely aware that she's out there, whatever she is and wherever she's from, and she'll be hungry again soon. I relive the whole mess whenever I shut my eyes, so sleep deprivation is my new American Dream.

The worst part, when I eventually pass out and the movie in my head starts, is that I should've known. I saw, but didn't believe. She wasn't sprayed green, she *was* green. Green as green can be.

Pies

I am a woman of faith and I am not going to apologize for that. You can call me "old-fashioned" if it suits you, because I am not ashamed to be a Christian and a Republican and a housewife and mother. We're the backbone of America and backbones are always in fashion, so don't even start with any of that "you wish Ronald Reagan was still president" and "you think you're always right" nonsense. Ronald Reagan was a fine man, and any person who holds an opinion that they don't think is right is insane (or on drugs).

I serve on the PTA, the Friends of the Library board, and the local hospital auxiliary, but my true love - my real love - is the church. I have a been a member of the Rosary Guild since I turned eighteen and I will go to my grave making pies.

That's right, pies. Twice a year, we have a huge bake sale to support the missions in Africa and Central America. Every time, there's a line at the table to buy my pies: dutch apple, peach, strawberry, chocolate supreme, even the lemon meringue. The years pass, children grow and leave the nest, neighbors change, jobs come and go, but everybody in this town has shared an appreciation of my pies - and that is not the sin of pride talking. Every slice is an opportunity to grow closer to God.

Go ahead and roll your eyes if you like. My grandmother explained it in a way that made perfect sense to me: the lower crust is prayer, supporting you through what life hands you, the filling is the mess you make of things, and the upper crust or topping is God pressing down, hearing your prayers and managing the whole precarious business. Not only do I think that's right overall, it's certainly been true in my life. Suffering is part of our salvation; it's necessary for us to turn to God in humility. And there's nothing like other human beings to help you save yourself, to help you suffer. There is no perfection outside of the Creator.

Growing up, my brother Lawrence got into all kinds of trouble with money and women and crime. He caused my parents endless sleepless nights. One evening, when he'd been missing for four days, he crawled in through my bedroom window deep at night to steal my stereo and my piggy bank. The smell of him woke me up and I screamed. He punched me right in the face - hard! He kept punching me until most of my front teeth were just a memory. My own brother. High on something, naturally. Weak and violent and too proud to turn to the Lord.

He came round many months later, when my teeth had been fixed. Wormed his way up to me and offered a bleary-eyed apology. I felt my heart harden and begged God to help me forgive. I went into the kitchen and spent some time praying and baking him a pie. I figured it would help us both in the end; besides, he was thin as a rail and I knew he'd gobble it up. We parted right with each other.

He didn't show up for work for two days and one of his friends went over to the trailer to see what was up - found both he and his girlfriend dead. Apparent overdose of some kind; they had enough bags of withered plant life and white powder to kill the whole town. Easy as ... well ... pie ... to guess what had happened. Did you know that fresh rhubarb is so tart that it will hide the taste of rat poison entirely?

I'm sorry; I didn't mean to alarm you. No, don't try to get up; you'll fall - and I'm not a young woman anymore, so I can't lift you back into the chair. Leaving you in a pile on the floor would be so rude! I'd feel terrible. Don't be scared now; the tongue goes to sleep first so that talking is impossible. You had the blueberry, Dear; that's the one with the horse tranquilizers. We have a bit before you lose muscle control and drift off to sleep. You're right with God, aren't you, Sugar?

You see, the way I look at it, I'm helping God keep a lid on things. Jesus, well, he's still trying to pull the right strings to spread His word, and God the Father has his hands full controlling the Muslims. The Holy Spirit is just fluttering all around us, asking us to lift up our hearts, and Mary, she and I are making pies. We have to bring the people back around to a place where they can look God in the eye and ...

I get long-winded. I know I do. I'm sorry. Luckily, I've made so many pies in my lifetime, I can "multi-task". Brian used to give me the hardest time about how I prattled on but, in the beginning, he used to love the sound of my voice (said it was music to his ears). Then came the children, the work promotions, and his growing inability to listen at all. He started coming home later and later and ... you know this story; everybody knows this story. Took up with a hostess at the golf club half his age, started working out, and got a Florida tan. He was generous in the divorce. I kept our house and got a good alimony settlement since I'd stayed home to raise our kids instead of climbing a corporate ladder for myself.

Brian and Tammy moved into a nice bungalow on the other side of town. They played tennis and had cocktail parties and were the very picture of health until the party.

Remember that I told you about my brother Lawrence? He once showed me how to pick a lock with a hair pin. Once inside the house, I injected a cyanide solution into their artificial sweetener packets, which they kept in a big bowl on the counter (God forbid they gain a pound using real butter or actual sugar). Emptying the syringe wet everything down, but it dried almost instantly. Apparently, when some friends arrived after work, Tammy made up a big pitcher of margaritas with extra sweetener and was carrying it out to the pool when the one she'd drank in the kitchen did its thing.

The authorities had sense enough to test the pitcher and found traces of poison; they arrested Brian immediately afterwards. I'm sure he spent a fortune on his defense attorney, but you don't need lots of money in jail anyway. He'll never get out, poor dear. On the bright side, he'll have lots of time to read the Bible and repent his sins. Lots of time.

You're getting sleepy. I understand. Here, I'm going to use this scarf to tie you to the chair; that way, you won't fall.

As I've said, I've made an incredible amount of pies in my lifetime. I'm tired now. My doctor tells me that I have a tumor lying between my intestines and my stomach and there's nothing they can do. I opted out of surgery and anything beyond basic chemotherapy. What's most important to me is that I finish the work I've begun - that I fulfill the obligations of my last mission bake sale.

There's a pecan pie for Jessie Dixon, who I know for a fact is as queer as the day is long. The sugar-roasted nuts will disguise the arsenic nicely.

There's a pan of blackberry cobbler for Ramona Samuel. I understand that some hard times feel like they might never end, but that is no excuse for helping yourself to the big bills in the collection plate. I was pleased at how the mandrake boiled right down to nothing in the syrup.

A strawberry mousse for Emma Fenton, bless her soul. She's losing her own battle with cancer, and deserves nothing more than to be lifted on a cloud of joy straight to God himself. I think I used two hundred and ninety nine of the three hundred anti-depressants the doctor gave me. I saved only one for myself (to take the edge off).

I'll work my shift at the table, then go out to my car and get my lunchbox out of the trunk. I have a special slice of dutch apple in reserve for myself. Apple is my favorite; it's so wholesome and simple, yet, with one bite, Eve consigned human nature to oblivion. There's a feeling of everything coming full circle.

I'll go to the altar of Our Lady and pray, then eat my pie. The caramel-and-graham cracker crust is so gooey that it'll be easy to forget about the morphine.

Then I'll sleep, just like you're sleeping now. Rest in peace, Honey. I forgive you for trying to steal my recipes.

About the Author

Tansy Undercrypt is a dark fiction writer living in the grim wilds of Minnesota. In addition to her writing, she is an accomplished illustrator, stage performer, and voice actor. "Small Towns, Dark Places" is her first published collection. Thank you for reading it.

Made in the USA
Lexington, KY
20 February 2013